Mr. Hynde Is Out Of His Mind!

My Weird School #6

Mr. Hynde Is Out Of His Mind!

Dan Gutman

Pictures by
Jim Paillot

HarperTrophy®
An Imprint of HarperCollinsPublishers

Library of Congress Cataloging-in-Publication Data

Gutman, Dan.

Mr. Hynde is out of his mind! / Dan Gutman ; pictures by Jim Paillot.— 1st HarperTrophy ed.

p.   cm. — (My weird school ; #6)

Summary: When boring Mr. Loring retires, A.J.'s class gets a new music teacher who raps, break-dances, and thinks he has what it takes to become a famous musician.

ISBN 0-06-074520-7 (pbk.) — ISBN 0-06-074521-5 (lib. bdg.)

[1. Schools—Fiction.   2. Musicians—Fiction.   3. Teachers—Fiction.   4. Learning—Fiction.   5. Humorous stories.]   I. Title: Mister Hynde is out of his mind!   II. Paillot, Jim, ill.   III. Title.   IV. Series.

PZ7.G9846Mq 2005   2004021508

[Fic]—dc22

11 12 13   LP/CW   20 19 18

❖

First Edition

To Emma

Contents

Boring, Snoring Mr. Loring

My name is A.J. and I hate school.

I hate reading.

I hate writing.

I hate arithmetic.

But there's one horrible subject that I *really* hate more than anything else.

Music.

Music is so dumb! Music is the most

1

boring subject in the history of the world. Why do we need music class in school, anyway? It's not like I'm going to grow up to be a singer. When I grow up, I'm going to be a professional dirt bike racer.

In first grade last year, the music teacher, Mr. Loring, made us sing all these totally corny songs from prehistoric times, like "Row, Row, Row Your Boat" and "Michael, Row the Boat Ashore." Mr. Loring loves boats, I guess. He's weird.

He's about a million hundred years old, and he has long gray hair. Mr. Loring told us that when he was a kid back in the last century, TV wasn't even invented yet. Can you imagine living in a world without TV? It must have been horrible! I would die if I didn't have TV.

Mr. Loring's favorite song for us to sing was "Who Stole the Cookie from the Cookie Jar?" You know the song:

Who stole the cookie from the cookie jar?
A.J. stole the cookie from the cookie jar.
Who me?
Yes you.
Couldn't be.
Then who?
Ryan stole the cookie from the cookie jar.

I used to like that song, but Mr. Loring made us sing it so many times that I never wanted to eat another cookie for the rest of my life.

Mr. Loring's other favorite song was "Five Little Monkeys Jumping on the Bed." That song got really old too. If any monkeys ever jumped on *my* bed, I would sell the bed. That's disgusting! I don't even like it when my sister jumps on my bed. Forget about monkeys.

"Everybody line up!" said my teacher, Miss Daisy, after we finished pledging the allegiance.

"Line up for what?" we all asked.

"It's time to go to music," Miss Daisy said.

"Yippee!" said Andrea Young, this really annoying girl with curly brown hair.

"Boo!" said just about everybody else. Nobody except Andrea and her friend Emily wanted to go see boring, snoring Mr. Loring.

Andrea loves everything about school. She even loves homework. One day

Andrea asked Miss Daisy if we could have *more* homework! Can you imagine asking your teacher to give you more homework?

Andrea is weird.

Goody Two-Shoes Andrea

Miss Daisy let Andrea (the little brown-noser) be the line leader when we walked down the hall to the music room. Her little crybaby friend Emily was the door holder. I walked with my pals Ryan and Michael.

We had just turned the corner outside

our classroom when I saw the most horrible thing in the history of the world. It was a sign on the wall by the office:

NEXT WEEK IS TV TURNOFF WEEK!

DON'T FORGET TO TURN OFF YOUR TV!

"Oh no!" Ryan groaned. "Say it's not true!"

"I'll die without TV!" said Michael. "TV Turnoff Week is the worst week of the year!"

"It's the worst week in the history of the world," I said.

"What are we going to do all week without TV?" asked Ryan.

"I might go crazy," said Michael.

It was even worse than we thought. The sign said that TV Turnoff Week had been such a success last year that they decided to make it TV Turnoff *Month* this year! Four whole weeks with no TV!

"Guys, this is the end of the world as we know it," I said.

"Oh, you boys are silly," Andrea said. "TV is for silly dumbheads anyway. I never watch TV. I'd rather spend my time singing or playing a musical instrument."

Andrea takes violin lessons and piano lessons and dancing lessons and singing lessons and just about every other kind of dumb lessons they have. If they give lessons in *anything*, Andrea takes them. If they gave lessons in how to take lessons, Andrea would probably take *them*.

"My mother told me that music cleans the soul," she said as we walked past the art room.

"Maybe you should try taking a bath," I said.

Ryan and Michael laughed at my funny joke.

"A.J., you wouldn't be so mean if you tried singing instead of sitting around watching TV all the time," Andrea said. "I love to sing. I can sing all the songs from *Annie*. That's my favorite movie."

Ugh.

Then Andrea started singing that song

about the sun coming out tomorrow. It was horrible. The police should use Andrea's singing to punish criminals in jail.

"Can you sing solo?" I asked Andrea when she finally stopped.

"Sure I can," she said.

"Then why don't you sing *so low* we can't hear you?"

Ryan and Michael cracked up at my funny joke. They are true friends.

"You're mean!" Andrea said.

"Please hold your tongue, A.J.," said Miss Daisy. Then she told me to be quiet because she knew that I was going to stick my tongue out and hold it.

Finally we got to the music room. Mr. Loring wasn't there yet, so Miss Daisy told us to sit on the rug.

Last year my first-grade teacher told us to sit Indian style, but she got in trouble because some Indian people didn't like it.

So she told us to sit like pretzels instead. Miss Daisy doesn't tell us to sit like Indians or like pretzels. She just says, "Crisscross applesauce," which doesn't mean anything at all.

I sat in the second row next to Ryan and Michael. Andrea and Emily sat in the

front row, of course. Miss Daisy said we could talk quietly until Mr. Loring arrived.

"Remember when Mr. Loring had us sing 'Jingle Bells'?" Michael asked.

"Yeah?"

"What's a bobtail?" Michael asked. "You sing 'bells on bobtail ring,' but I never knew what a bobtail was."

"Beats me," said Ryan.

"I think a bobtail is a kind of car," I guessed.

"Nobody names a car Bobtail," said Michael.

"Bob backward is still Bob," Ryan said. "And tuna backward is a nut."

"Tuba backward is a butt," I said.

"I used to have a fish named Fred," said Ryan.

"What does that have to do with bob-tails?" asked Michael.

Nothing," Ryan said. "I was just think-ing about Fred."

Suddenly that goody two-shoes Andrea turned around.

"You boys are dumbheads," she said. "A bobtail is a little furry animal with a short tail. Everybody knows that."

She was probably right, but I don't like Andrea Young telling me anything. She started singing "Jingle Bells."

"Who asked you?" I interrupted. "You don't know anything about music."

"Do too!" Andrea said, all mad. "I've been playing the piano ever since I was four years old."

"Don't you get tired?" I asked.

I thought that was a pretty funny joke, but nobody laughed. Can't win 'em all.

"I can even play a Beethoven sonata," Andrea bragged, all proud of herself.

"You play with Beethoven's snot?" I said. "That's disgusting!"

Andrea got all huffy and turned back around. Why doesn't a piano fall on her head?

"Boy, Mr. Loring is really late," Michael said.

"Maybe he died of old age," said Ryan.

"I think *we're* going to die of old age waiting for him," I said.

"Maybe he bored himself to death," said Michael.

"You boys are mean!" said that crybaby Emily. "Mr. Loring is *nice*!"

She looked like she was going to cry. What a baby! My mom says that all you have to do to get some people upset is to look at them sideways. I tried looking at Emily sideways, but she didn't even notice.

Miss Daisy told us she was going to the office to see what happened to Mr. Loring. She told us to be on our best behavior while she was gone. So as soon as she left the room, me and Michael and Ryan got up and shook our butts at the class. Most of the kids laughed.

That's when the most amazing thing in the history of the world happened.

The One-Man Funky Groove Machine

3

First this weird purple smoke started pouring out on the floor in the front of the music room. Then the sound of drums started pounding out of a boom box on Mr. Loring's desk. Then the lights went out and these laser beams started shooting around the music room in all different colors. It was cool!

Suddenly two men ran into the room and started dancing around. They were wearing football jerseys and baseball caps and holding microphones.

"Ooh, hats aren't allowed in school," I heard Andrea say to Emily. "Those men are going to get in trouble."

One of the guys started clapping his hands over his head to the drumbeat. The other one yelled into his microphone.

"Are you ready for some music class?" the guy screamed.

We all looked at one another. We're not supposed to yell in school. But Miss Daisy wasn't there, so I figured it was okay.

"Yeah!" I yelled.

"I SAID, 'ARE YOU READY FOR SOME MUSIC CLASS?'" the guy repeated.

"Yeah!" everybody yelled.

"Are you ready to get down?" the guy screamed.

"We're already down!" somebody yelled.

"And now, second graders . . . appearing live and in person at Ella Mentry School . . . is the one . . . the only . . . Jam Master Hynde, the One-Man Funky Groove Machine! Give it up, y'all! 'Cause Mr. Hynde is in the house!"

The two guys ran out the door. The

drums got louder. The lights got brighter. Andrea and Emily put their hands over their ears.

That's when Mr. Hynde ran in the door. He was a lot younger than Mr. Loring. He had on a baseball cap too, and he was wearing this big purple cape with sequins all over it. He had on sunglasses, too, even though he was inside. I guess that was to protect his eyes from the laser beams.

"Ooh, he's really cute!" all the girls said.

"Put your hands together!" Mr. Hynde screamed. "I said, 'PUT YOUR HANDS TOGETHER!'"

We all started clapping. Mr. Hynde

danced around awhile, and then he threw off his purple cape and started rapping to the beat:

"Old Mr. Loring he was over the hill.
So the board of education told him he
would have to chill.
My name is Hynde, and I'm gonna blow
your mind.
I ain't no music teacher, I'm a born music
creature.
'Cause my daddy's name was Amos, but
he never became famous.
So he took me on his lap, and he taught
me how to rap.
I can rhyme any line. I got juice like
Dr. Seuss.

Until I hit it big, I got this teaching gig.
So sit back on your pants and dig my new
break dance."

Mr. Hynde got down on the floor and started spinning around on his back like a top. Then he started spinning on his head!

It was cool.

Finally the music and lasers stopped, and the regular lights came back on. Mr. Hynde took off his sunglasses and put on regular glasses. He was panting like a dog after a hard game of fetch.

Me and Ryan and Michael got up and gave him a standing ovation, and the rest of the class joined in too.

Well, everybody except for Andrea and Emily. They just sat there, with their mouths open and their eyes all big like they just saw an alien spaceship or something.

"Yo, what up, homeys?" asked Mr. Hynde.

"Are you our new music teacher?" asked Michael.

"True that!" said Mr. Hynde. "What do you think I am, brother, your dentist? Welcome to music, second grade! I'm here to rock your world."

"I liked Mr. Loring," Andrea whined.

Nah-nah-nah boo-boo on her! Finally there was something at school that Andrea didn't like.

Anything Andrea doesn't like, I like. And anything Andrea likes, I don't like. We never agree on anything. I didn't even like rap music very much, but I think I'm gonna like it now that I know Andrea hates it.

Andrea and Emily started in brown-nosing Mr. Hynde right away. They were trying to act all cute.

"What musical instruments do you play, Mr. Hynde?" asked Andrea.

"Sister, I play turntable," Mr. Hynde said.

Then he took one of those big old black records that my parents used to listen to in ancient times. He put it on a record player. Then he started sliding the record back and forth while he rubbed the needle against it. These weird sounds came out of the boom box. It was cool.

"Scratching records will ruin them," Andrea said. "You should hold records by the edges so they don't get scratched."

"Can you possibly be any more boring?" I asked her.

"Mr. Hynde," asked Emily, "do you know how to sing the doe a deer song? That's my favorite song."

"No problemo, sister," said Mr. Hynde. And then he started rapping again:

"Doe a deer and deer a doe.
The deer is here and the deer is near.
But the doe she gotta go.

'Cause the doe is in a show.

And that doe she is a pro.

That's why she gotta blow.

I hate to tell ya, Joe.

But that doe got run over by a buffalo

So that doe ain't never gonna be no deer.

And that's the story of doe a deer."

Me and Ryan and Michael gave Mr. Hynde another standing ovation.

"That's not doe a deer!" Emily complained. "That's a sad song about a deer that died!"

She looked like she was going to cry, like always.

"Chill, sister," said Mr. Hynde. "It's just a song."

"Yeah, chill," I told Emily.

Andrea said she knew the real doe a deer song, and she started singing it. But she only got up to the part about the drop of golden sun when Mr. Hynde held up his hand like a police officer telling you to stop your car.

"Whoa, that stuff is old school, sister," he told Andrea. "It's so yesterday."

"I like Mr. Hynde's doe a deer song better," I said.

"Me too!" agreed most of the other kids.

"Aren't we going to learn about all the great composers," Andrea whined, "like Beethoven and Mozart and Gershwin and Irving Berlin?"

"Those dudes didn't boogie," said Mr.

Hynde. "I never listen to that stuff. *This* year in music class I'm gonna teach you how to get down and get your swerve on! We're gonna bust a move!"

"I don't think I'm going to like music class this year," Andrea whispered to Emily with a big worried face.

I think I'm gonna *love* music class this year!

The Plot to Get Rid of Mr. Hynde

4

"Mr. Hynde is the coolest teacher in the history of the world," I told the guys.

We were sitting around the vomitorium eating lunch. I traded my peach to Ryan for his cookies because food that has hair on it is disgusting. Ryan will eat anything, though. Once he even ate a bug.

"He doesn't act like a music teacher at all," said Michael.

"The best part is, we'll never have to sing that dumb cookie jar song again!" Ryan said. We all did a big high five over that.

At the next table, I could hear Andrea and Emily moaning and complaining about Mr. Hynde.

"He's really cute, and he's a pretty good singer," Emily said. "But he doesn't even play any musical instruments. How can you be a music teacher when you don't play a musical instrument?"

"He has no right to be teaching music," Andrea said. "I'm going to ask my mom to talk to Principal Klutz. Maybe she can get Mr. Hynde fired."

Me and Michael and Ryan turned around at that.

"What?!" we shouted.

"Mr. Hynde is a terrible music teacher," Andrea said. "My mom is the PTA vice president, and she said that if enough parents complain about a teacher, they can get the teacher fired."

It figured that the school finally replaced that old dinosaur Mr. Loring with somebody cool and Andrea would start complaining. What is her problem?

"I think Mr. Hynde is incompetent," Andrea said.

"He wears diapers?" I asked.

"Not in*con*tinent, dumbhead!" Andrea said. "In*com*petent! It means he doesn't do a good job."

"Yeah," said Emily.

That Emily agrees with everything Andrea says. She's so annoying. I decided to yank her crank.

"Maybe Mr. Hynde isn't a music teacher at all," I told her. "Did you ever think of that?"

"What do you mean?" Emily asked.

"I mean maybe Mr. Loring wasn't fired. Maybe Mr. Hynde kidnapped him and stuffed him in a piano and dumped it in the river. Stuff like that happens all the time, you know."

Emily looked worried, like I wasn't even kidding. That girl will fall for anything.

"We've got to *do* something!" Emily said. Then she went running out of the vomitorium.

Emily is weird.

Mr. Hynde
Gets Funky

5

If Andrea and her mother got Mr. Hynde fired, it would be a horrible disaster. I was determined to stop them. But in the meantime, I had another problem to worry about.

Multiplication.

We were just starting to learn about

multiplication, and I didn't get it. I understood how 2 plus 2 equals 4. But then how was it possible for 2 *times* 2 to equal 4 too? I mean, 3 plus 3 and 3 *times* 3 don't equal the same number. It just didn't make sense.

The way I looked at it, if 2 plus 2 equals 4, and 2 times 2 also equals 4, then addition and multiplication were the same thing. And if they were the same thing, why did we have to learn *both* of them? I was having a tough enough time with addition

$2+2=4$

$2\times2=4$

and subtraction before this multiplication stuff messed everything up.

I asked Miss Daisy to explain how 2 plus 2 and 2 times 2 can both equal 4.

"How should I know?" she replied. "I don't know anything about math."

Miss Daisy is crazy!

"Everybody line up," Miss Daisy said after we finished putting away our math books.

"Line up for what?"

"It's time for music with Mr. Hynde," Miss Daisy said.

"Yippee!" shouted me and Michael and Ryan.

"Boo!" said Andrea and Emily.

"Andrea, I thought you loved music," Miss Daisy said. "You've been playing piano ever since you were four."

"She must be really tired," I said. Nobody laughed at my joke again, but I didn't care. I'm going to keep telling that joke until somebody laughs.

"Mr. Hynde doesn't play music," Andrea said. "He just makes noise."

"Well, we have to go to music anyway," said Miss Daisy.

Nah-nah-nah boo-boo on Andrea! I hate her.

We went to the music room in single file. This girl Annette was the line leader. Andrea and Emily were at the end of the line, which was a first in the history of the world. They always want to get everywhere before anyone else.

The music room was empty. But suddenly Mr. Hynde swept in and threw off his cape.

"Should we sit like pretzels, Mr. Hynde?" somebody asked.

"No way, homeys," Mr. Hynde said. "You sit for reading and writing and arithmetic. In music you get up and shake your booty! The only way to get down is to get up!"

Mr. Hynde jumped around like a lunatic, and so did we. It was cool.

"Okay, my little peeps," Mr. Hynde said.

"Today we're gonna learn about percussion. Which one of you shorties can tell me what percussion is?"

I raised my hand and Mr. Hynde called on me.

"Percussion is when you say bad words," I said.

"That's cussin', brother," Mr. Hynde said. "Andrea?"

"Percussion is when one object hits against another object," she said, all proud of herself.

"Word up, Andrea!" Mr. Hynde said.

Andrea thinks she knows everything. I'd like to percussion her with a stick.

"Listen up," Mr. Hynde said. He picked

up two rulers from his desk and started hitting things with them. He hit his desk. He hit the chalkboard. He hit the window. He hit his coffee mug.

"You hear how each object makes a different sound?" Mr. Hynde asked.

"That's not music," Andrea said. "It's just noise!"

"Oh, that's cold, girl!" Mr. Hynde said. "Sister, anything can be musical."

Mr. Hynde started running around the room, drumming on everything in sight with the rulers. He's a good drummer! Then he put his foot inside a garbage can and started tap-dancing around the room while he kept whacking things with the rulers. He's a good tap dancer, too.

It was getting noisy! Andrea and Emily put their hands over their ears. Mr. Hynde started making weird drumming sounds with his mouth while he was

whacking things with the rulers and tap-dancing with the garbage can on his foot.

It was cool. Everybody except for Andrea and Emily was dancing around. Mr. Hynde started hitting his butt on an empty desk while he was making weird drumming sounds with his mouth and whacking things with the rulers and tap-dancing with the garbage can.

Mr. Hynde is out of his mind!

He was doing all those things at the same time when suddenly, the most amazing thing in the history of the world happened.

The door to the music room opened. And who do you think walked in?

It was Mr. Klutz, the school principal!

"Oh, snap!" said Mr. Hynde.

Mr. Klutz is completely bald. I mean, he has no hair at all on his head.

Everything stopped. Mr. Hynde stood there like a statue. A statue with a garbage can on its foot. Everybody stopped dancing. There was no noise at all. We were all looking at Mr. Klutz as he stood in the doorway.

You should have been there. It was unbearable! We didn't know what to say. We didn't know what to do. I had to think fast.

Finally I said, "Mr. Hynde is teaching us cussin'."

"Is that so?" Principal Klutz asked.

"Percussion," said Mr. Hynde.

"Mr. Hynde is hitting things and making way too much noise," said Andrea. "He calls that music."

Principal Klutz walked over to Mr. Hynde.

"Is that true, Mr. Hynde?" asked Principal Klutz.

Nobody said a word. Nobody made a sound. I thought I was gonna die.

"True that, sir, I'm afraid it is," said Mr. Hynde. He took his foot out of the garbage can.

"He's damaging school property and causing a disturbance," said Andrea. "Are you going to fire him?" She had this evil smile on her face.

All the kids looked at Mr. Klutz. Mr. Klutz looked at Mr. Hynde. Mr. Hynde looked at Mr. Klutz. And then Mr. Klutz did the most amazing thing in the history of the world. He started rapping:

"Mr. Hynde is phat. I'm down with that.
Even kids who are Russian gotta learn
about percussion.
So make some noise, you little girls and
boys.
I rule the school. And I say Mr. Hynde is
cool.
In school I'm king, and I say do your own
thing.

Now watch me groove 'cause I can bust a move."

Then Mr. Klutz did a little dance and spun on the floor on his back.

Mr. Klutz is nuts!

With Principal Klutz still sitting on the floor, Mr. Hynde came up behind him and started drumming the top of his bald head like it was a bongo.

It was amazing! You should have been there. It was almost even better than watching TV.

Everybody except Andrea and Emily started clapping. Mr. Klutz got up and said he had to go back to his office and do some important principal stuff.

"Please continue to, uh, get down and funky with your bad self," said Mr. Klutz. "Peace out."

And then he left.

You should have seen the look on Andrea's face when Mr. Hynde was playing bongos on our principal's head! I guess she's not going to get Mr. Hynde fired after all.

Ha-ha-ha. It was the greatest thing that ever happened in the history of the world.

I hate her.

6

Beauty and the Beast

I really missed TV.

TV Turnoff Month started, and I had to go a whole day without any TV. It was horrible! I thought I was gonna die!

Believe it or not, I couldn't wait for school to start. There's a TV in our classroom, but we hardly ever get to watch it, so at least I wasn't missing anything.

Plus, we had music class. And music class with Mr. Hynde is better than TV anyway.

"Good news, my little shorties," Mr. Hynde said. "In honor of TV Turnoff Month, we're gonna put on a play!"

"Yippee!" shouted all the girls. "Plays are fun."

"Boo!" moaned all the boys. "Plays are dumb."

"This play's gonna be off the hook, dudes," Mr. Hynde told us. "It's gonna be a hip-hop play."

"I was in a play at day camp last summer," said Andrea. "It was called *The*

Princess and the Pea. I played the beautiful princess."

"Did you pee right on the stage?" I asked. "That's disgusting!"

"Not *that* kind of pea, A.J.!"

"We're gonna put on *Beauty and the Beast,*" said Mr. Hynde. "Now who wants to be Beauty?"

"I do! I do! I do!" shouted Andrea and a few of the other girls.

Mr. Hynde did eeny meeny minie moe, and guess which smarty-pants brown-noser little Miss Perfect who should have a refrigerator fall on her head won?

"Okay, Andrea is the beauty," said Mr. Hynde. "Now which one of you little dudes wants to be the beast?"

None of us boys raised his hand. No way I was going to be some dumb beast in a dumb play.

"Don't bail on me, brothers," Mr. Hynde said. "*One* of you homeboys has to be the beast or we can't have the play."

I looked over at Ryan and Michael. They were both looking at the floor and had their arms folded across their chests.

"We don't want to be in a play," Ryan said.

"Oh, I forgot to clue you," Mr. Hynde said. "The beast gets to lock Beauty in a dungeon and torture her."

"I'll be the beast!" I shouted before

anybody else could get his hand in the air.

"Okay, A.J. is the beast," Mr. Hynde said.

This play is going to be cool!

7

K-i-s-s-i-n-g

Me and Ryan and Michael were sitting around the playground at recess. Michael was looking through the script for the play that Mr. Hynde gave me.

"Did you read this, A.J.?" Michael asked.

"Nah," I said, "reading is boring."

"Well, you might want to read this,"

Michael said. "It says here that the beast has to kiss Beauty."

"What?! Let me see that!" I grabbed the script. He was right! It said it right there on the last page.

Beauty and the beast kiss.

"Oooooh!" Ryan said. "A.J. and Andrea are in *love*!"

"Shut up!" I said. "I thought I just had to lock her in a dungeon."

"First you lock her in a dungeon," Michael said. "In the end you fall in love and you've got to kiss her."

"That's disgusting!" I said. "I wouldn't kiss Andrea if they paid me a million dollars."

"You're gonna have to," Michael said. "And nobody's gonna pay you a dime."

Then Michael and Ryan started singing:

"A.J. and Andrea sitting in a tree
k-i-s-s-i-n-g!
First comes love, then comes marriage.
Then comes A.J. with a baby carriage!"

If those guys weren't my best friends, I would really hate them.

"I won't do it!" I said. "I'll run away someplace where they'll never find me."

Michael and Ryan sang the dumb kissing song again, so I left. I was really mad.

I didn't exactly know where to run to. I figured I'd go to the boys' room and hang out in there for a while.

But on the way to the boys' room, I passed the music room. The door was closed, but there's a little window in the door. I stood on my tiptoes and looked inside. Mr. Hynde was in there.

I put my ear against the door. I could hear a drum machine, and Mr. Hynde was rapping, too. I couldn't make out the words. I opened the door.

"Yo, Beast!" Mr. Hynde said. "You the man! How's it hangin', brother?"

"Okay, I guess," I said. "What are you doing?"

"Layin' down some beats," Mr. Hynde said. "I'm workin' on my own CD."

"Cool!" I said. "Are you gonna be a famous rapper?"

"Word up, cuz," Mr. Hynde said. "Maybe someday I'll be a star and you can say I used to be your music teacher. Hey, you want my autograph? Once I get famous, I might not sign 'em anymore."

"No thanks," I said.

"What's the matter, Beast?" said Mr. Hynde. "You bummed out 'cause you can't watch TV?"

"No, I've got a problem, Mr. Hynde."

"Be straight," he said. "You can tell me."

"I don't want to be the beast."

"Why not, dude?" Mr. Hynde asked. "The beast is the man! The beast rules!"

"I don't want to kiss Andrea Young," I admitted.

"Ohhhh," Mr. Hynde said. "Kissin' is gross, eh? 'Fraid you'll get cooties?"

"Well, yeah."

"Let me clue you, brother," said Mr. Hynde. "Kissin' girls is fly. Someday all you're gonna wanna do is kiss girls.

Someday, when you wanna kiss a girl, that girl might not wanna kiss you. It's kinda like gettin' my autograph. You should do it now, 'cause you might not have the chance later. Besides, it's just a play. It doesn't mean you like her."

"But Andrea is horrible and disgusting!"

Mr. Hynde sat down at his desk.

"A.J., when I was a little shortie like you, I thought green beans were horrible and disgusting," he said. "But my mama said I had to eat 'em. She told me to pretend the green beans were somethin' I really liked. So I pretended they were oatmeal cookies. Then they didn't taste so bad. See what I mean?"

"I don't like oatmeal cookies," I said.

"Well, what *do* you like?" Mr. Hynde asked.

I thought about it for a minute.

"I like dirt bikes," I said. "When I grow up, I'm gonna be a dirt bike racer."

"So pretend Andrea is a dirt bike," he suggested.

"Huh?"

"Go ahead, give it a shot," Mr. Hynde said. "We need you in there. You're my beast, dude. Nobody else can be the beast. You're the beast from the east."

"Well, okay," I said.

I still didn't know if I'd be able to kiss Andrea without throwing up.

The Play

For the next week, the second grade rehearsed and rehearsed and rehearsed the play. After school I went home and rehearsed my lines some more. I couldn't turn on the TV anyway, so it was good to have something to do.

In school we rehearsed the whole play

from start to finish. It was fun torturing Andrea. The only part we didn't rehearse was the kissing part. Mr. Hynde said we would save that for the real show on Friday night.

Ryan and Michael couldn't believe that I was really going to kiss Andrea. I told them that Mr. Hynde said it wouldn't be so horrible if I pretended she was a dirt bike.

"I wouldn't kiss a dirt bike," Ryan said.

"Well, what *would* you kiss?" I asked.

"I really like football," Ryan said. "I'd kiss a football."

Ryan is weird.

Finally the night of the big show

arrived. Everybody was dressed up in his or her costume. We peeked through the curtains in the multipurpose room and saw all the parents were there. I was nervous. Mr. Hynde told us everything was going to be fine.

We were waiting for the curtain to open when Andrea pulled me aside.

"A.J.," she said, "I want you to know that just because we have to kiss each other doesn't mean I like you."

"I don't like you, either," I said.

"Good," she said. "I'm glad we agree on something."

"Kissing girls is gross," I told her.

"Kissing boys is gross too," she said. "I

even went to Mr. Hynde and told him I didn't want to be in the play because I didn't want to kiss you."

"So did I!"

"He told me I should pretend that you're something I really like," Andrea said.

"That's what he told me!" I said. "I'm going to pretend you're a dirt bike."

"I'm going to pretend you're an encyclopedia," Andrea said.

"Fine."

So we did the play. I remembered all my lines, and locking Andrea in the dungeon was fun. Everything was going great.

But the whole time, in the back of my mind, I was thinking that soon I would have to kiss Andrea. It was a horrible thought.

We were a minute away from the big kissing part. The whole cast was up on the stage.

Andrea was standing right next to me. I was really nervous.

Michael leaned over and whispered in my ear. "Remember, she's a dirt bike," he said.

Emily leaned over and whispered to Andrea. "Remember, he's an encyclopedia," she said.

And then, before I could catch my

breath, it was time. The big moment. The kiss.

I leaned over toward Andrea.

Andrea leaned over toward me.

My heart was beating fast. I closed my eyes.

Dirt bike. Dirt bike. Dirt bike. Dirt bike.

I was trying really hard to pretend that Andrea was a dirt bike.

And at that very moment, the most amazing thing in the

history of the world happened.

Andrea didn't kiss me.

I opened my eyes. Andrea had stepped up to the microphone at the front of the stage.

She started singing!

"'The sun will come out tomorrow . . .'" she sang.

She was singing that dumb stick-out-your-chin-and-grin song from that *Annie* movie! It wasn't even in the script!

"'Tomorrow! Tomorrow! I love you

tomorrow . . .'"

It was horrible and all, but it was still the greatest moment in my life because at least I didn't have to kiss Andrea.

All the parents were smiling and nodding their heads. When Andrea finished singing the dumb song, they all went crazy, clapping and cheering and whistling and stamping their feet. Andrea bowed, and the play was over.

"I'm sorry, A.J.," Andrea said to me during the standing ovation. "I just couldn't do it. I was afraid that if I kissed you, I might throw up."

"Thanks," I said. "Me too."

Andrea gave me a hug.

"Oooooh!" Ryan said, "A.J. and Andrea are in *love*!"

The audience was still clapping when we noticed Mr. Hynde at the side of the stage behind the curtain. He was crying!

We all ran over to him. Tears were streaming down his cheeks. I figured Mr. Hynde was upset because Andrea messed up his hip-hop play.

"What's wrong, Mr. Hynde?" Emily asked.

"What was that song?" he asked, wiping the tears with his sleeve.

"It's called 'Tomorrow,'" Andrea said. "It's from *Annie*."

"It's the most beautiful song I ever heard," Mr. Hynde said. And then he started crying again.

Mr. Hynde is weird.

TV, at Last

We were supposed to have music on Monday, but Mr. Hynde was absent. We were kind of worried. Maybe he was sick, or maybe a meteor hit his house or something. That stuff happens all the time. But Miss Daisy told us he was fine and that we shouldn't worry so much.

A few days later, after we finished pledging the allegiance, Principal Klutz made an announcement over the loud-speaker.

"Teachers, please turn on the TV sets in your rooms," he said.

We all gasped.

"But it's still TV Turnoff Month!" just about everybody in the whole school yelled.

"Forget about that!" Mr. Klutz said. "Turn on your TVs! There is a very special tape I need everyone to see."

Whatever Mr. Klutz wanted us to see must have been really important. Even before TV Turnoff Month, we were hardly ever allowed to watch TV during school. Miss Daisy went to the front of the class and turned on the TV.

It had been so long since I'd seen TV that I almost forgot what it looked like. But it didn't take me long to figure out what was on the screen.

It was this dumb show called *American Idol,* where people get up and sing dumb songs and these dumb judges tell them how bad they sing. People vote for them, and one by one the singers have to leave until there is a winner. Why the heck did Principal Klutz want us to watch *that*?

Some announcer guy said, "Our next contestant is a music teacher at the Ella

Mentry School—"

And out walked Mr. Hynde!

I just about fell out of my seat. Everybody in the class gasped.

We couldn't believe it! It was the most amazing thing that ever happened in the history of the world! You should have

been there. Our own Mr. Hynde was on TV!

"He's been working on his own rap CD," I told everybody.

"This is gonna be cool," said Ryan.

Mr. Hynde stepped up to the microphone. He looked a little nervous. Music started playing and Mr. Hynde started singing.

"'The sun will come out tomorrow. . . .'"

I wouldn't believe it! Mr. Hynde wasn't singing one of his rap songs. He was singing that dumb bet-your-bottom-dollar song! Tears were rolling down his cheeks while he sang.

"'Tomorrow . . . tomorrow . . .'"

After he finished the song, we all cheered. Even me, and I hate that dumb song. I thought the judges were going to say how terrible Mr. Hynde was, because they pretty much hate everybody. But they didn't. They said he was really good. And when it was announced that Mr. Hynde was going to advance to the next round, we all went crazy.

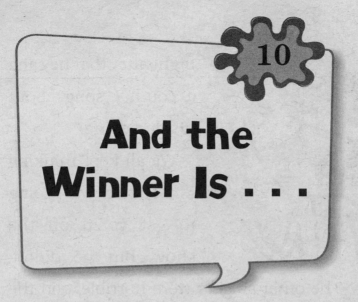

And the Winner Is . . .

Finally TV Turnoff Month ended and life went back to normal. I watched Mr. Hynde every night on that *American Idol* show. One night he sang a rap song. The next night he came out with a guitar and a crazy costume and sang a rock 'n' roll song. He could really play guitar! The night after that he sang a country song about his dog dying.

We all kept thinking Mr. Hynde was going to get voted off the show, but he didn't. The other singers were horrible, and the judges said really mean things to them. One by one, they were sent home.

Mr. Hynde's picture was in the newspaper. Everybody at school was talking about him.

We missed music class two weeks in a row because Mr. Hynde was working on the TV show. But we didn't mind. We were so proud of him.

Finally there were just two singers left. Mr. Hynde was one of them. The other one was this lady with a big nose. One of them was going to be the winner.

It all came down to Saturday night. Mr. Hynde sang a song, and then the lady with the big nose sang a song.

And guess what?

Well, I'm not even going to tell you because I don't want to. So nah-nah-nah boo-boo on you.

Okay, okay, that was mean. I'll tell you.

Mr. Hynde won! He really won! It was the greatest thing that ever happened in the history of the world!

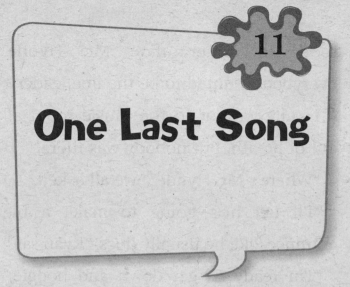

One Last Song

On Monday morning everybody came to school excited. We got even more excited when Miss Daisy told us to line up for music class.

"Yippee!" everybody yelled, even Emily and Andrea.

We couldn't wait to get to the music

89

room to congratulate Mr. Hynde. Everybody wanted to be the line leader.

Finally we got to the music room all out of breath. But nobody was there.

"Where's Mr. Hynde?" we all asked.

"I'll bet he's going to make a big entrance, like he usually does," Ryan said.

"I'm ready to get down and boogie," Michael said.

So we waited. And we waited and waited and waited. Finally, after about a million hundred years, the door opened. And you won't believe who walked in.

It was Mr. Loring!

Boring, snoring Mr. Loring was standing there, looking as boring as ever.

Everybody gasped.

"Sit down, please," Mr. Loring said. "We always sit down for music class."

"Mr. Loring!" Andrea asked. "What are *you* doing here?"

"I am here to teach music, of course," he said.

"What happened to Mr. Hynde?" I asked.

"Apparently he quit," said Mr. Loring.

"What?" I shouted. "That's not fair!"

"Principal Klutz asked me to come back," Mr. Loring said, "and I agreed, against my better judgment."

Everybody moaned. Mr. Loring reached into his jacket and pulled out a piece of paper.

"Mr. Hynde left a note for you," he said. "Would you like me to read it?"

"Yeah!"

So Mr. Loring read Mr. Hynde's note:

"I hope you dudes don't think I'm rude.
Don't moan and cry 'cause I didn't say
good-bye.
I had to keep it real 'til I got a record
deal.
But now I hit it big, so I quit my teaching
gig.
You kids are cool. I dig your school.
Wherever I go, whatever I do,
There's one thing true.
I'll always remember you."

Emily started crying, that crybaby.

Well, to be honest, we *all* started crying.

"I realize you're sad that Mr. Hynde is no longer here," said Mr. Loring. "Maybe if we sing a song, it will make you feel better."

"Can we sing that sun will come out tomorrow song?" I asked. "That will cheer us up."

"Yeah, it will remind us of Mr. Hynde," said Michael.

"I was thinking of something else," Mr. Loring said. And then he began to sing:

"Who stole the cookie from the cookie jar?
A.J. stole the cookie from the cookie jar.
Who me?
Yes you.
Couldn't be.
Then who?
Emily stole the cookie from the cookie jar."

No! Not *that* song! Anything but *that* song!

Mr. Loring made us sing that dumb cookie jar song over and over again until everybody's name in the whole class was mentioned. It was horrible. I thought I was gonna die.

Well, it looks like boring, snoring Mr. Loring is back at Ella Mentry School for the rest of the year. I guess we're just gonna have to put up with him until Mr. Klutz hires a new music teacher.

Like the song says, we'll have to stick out our chins and grin. We're gonna have to hang on till tomorrow, come what may.

But it won't be easy!